Doctor De Soto Goes To Africa

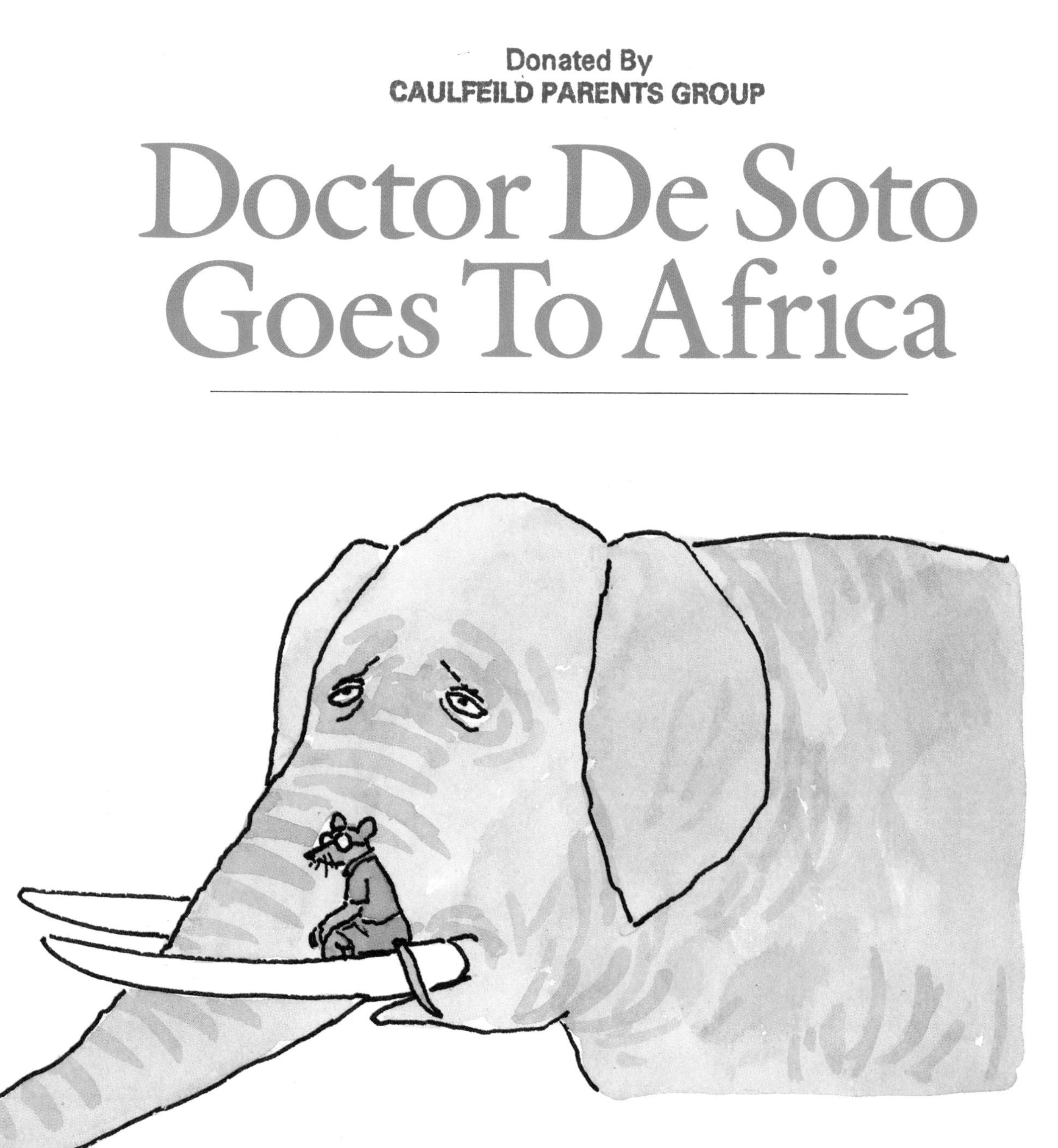

WILLIAM STEIG

Michael di Capua Books
HarperCollins Publishers

To Emma, Jonathan, Alicia, Jonas, Will, and Kate

Library of Congress catalog card number: 91-76414
Printed in the United States of America
Designed by Atha Tehon
First edition, 1992

Doctor Bernard De Soto was such a one-in-a-million, hum-dinger of a dentist that the whole world knew about him, and also about his wife, Deborah, who helped him work his wonders.

The two of them were listening to Caruso one evening when this cablegram arrived:

DR D SOTO BEG YOU COME DABWAN WEST AFRICA
AM ELEPHANT WITH UNBEARABLE TOOTHACHE
NO DENTIST HERE CAN HELP WILL PAY TEN THOUSAND
GOLD WALULUS PLEASE MUDAMBO

The De Sotos had never been in a foreign country or, for that matter, in an elephant's mouth. Mrs. De Soto sang out: "Let us go-oleo!" And her husband chimed in: "Yes, indeedle-de-doe!" After which they kissed and cabled back: WILL COME.

Just two days later, husband and wife were watching flying fish and spouting whales from cozy deck chairs. On their way to help a suffering elephant, they were enjoying the great ocean.

When the ship docked in Dabwan, the patient's brother, Adiba, was there waiting. He instantly recognized the De Sotos. They were the only mice coming down the gangplank.

Adiba introduced himself, then transported them, bag and baggage, to Mudambo's home.

Mudambo was so excited to see his saviors he could hardly speak. "Gah bless you bloth!" he blabbered.

It was 7 p.m. in that part of the world, so Mrs. Mudambo led them all in to dinner. Mudambo couldn't chew solid food. All he could manage was a gigantic aspirin washed down with warm coconut milk.

“I think we better skip dessert,” said Mrs. Mudambo. “My darling is in pain.”

Everyone trooped out to the garden, and Doctor De Soto, his wife right behind him, hurried up Mudambo’s trunk to study the tooth that had brought them all the way to Africa.

Doctor De Soto had never seen such a thoroughly rotten molar. No wonder no other dentist could deal with it!

"I'm confident I can reconstruct this wreck," he announced. "All I need is a piece of the tusk my wife is sitting on."

Mudambo was appalled. His tusks were his most admired feature. "Let me—*ouch*—think it—*wow*—over," he mumbled.

Mrs. Mudambo came up with a sensible suggestion. "What about that stuffed walrus in the Museum of Natural History?" she said. "It has gorgeous tusks. And just the right shade of ivory."

Everyone agreed that the Museum couldn't possibly refuse Mudambo a little piece of tusk. And neither could the walrus.

Adiba set off for the Museum, which stayed open late on Fridays, while Doctor De Soto got right to work. But even his most delicate touch couldn't keep Mudambo from yodeling with pain.

Mrs. De Soto always knew exactly which instrument her husband would need next.

Long past bedtime, there was still much to be done. The able dentist, his able assistant, and their unhappy patient decided to get some sleep and carry on at daybreak.

The De Sotos went to bed on Mrs. Mudambo's pincushion.

Around midnight, while his wife slept, Doctor Bernard De Soto was kidnapped. A hand covered his mouth, and he was hustled off in the clutches of a certain rhesus monkey, Honkitonk by name.

"Sir! What is *this*?" Doctor De Soto demanded as soon as his mouth was uncovered. "Where are you taking me?"

"Mind your own business," snarled the monkey.

(Honkitonk bore a grudge against Mudambo, who had referred to him, in public, as "a moron." He hadn't emigrated from India just to be insulted by an ill-bred pachyderm with a preposterous schnozzola. He wanted Mudambo to suffer!)

Honkitonk took the dentist to his secret hideout deep in the jungle, shoved him into a birdcage, and covered it with leaves.

"You have no legal right to do this!" Doctor De Soto cried. Honkitonk didn't respond. He just sauntered off, extremely pleased with himself.

"What a moron!" the dentist muttered. He tugged at the bars of the cage, trying to wrench them apart, but they refused to yield. All night long, he kept walking in circles and worrying—worrying about his dear Deborah. By now she must be frantic.

And indeed she was. She, too, was walking in circles. Had her beloved Bernard been eaten by some predator? By a hyena? Or a sneaky ocelot? Maybe swallowed, clothes and all, by a pitiless python?

Of course, Doctor De Soto was also worried about his patient. How was that poor soul faring? Poor Mudambo, his sore molar was more than he could bear. Occasionally, he'd fling himself to the floor and make the whole house rattle.

"Is anybody looking for me?" Doctor De Soto kept wondering.

All Dabwan was out looking—here, there, every which where. On the second day, and twice after that, he heard voices calling: "Doctor De-e So-o-o-to! Doctor Bern-a-a-ard De So-o-o-o-to!"

He yelled back, "I'm here! Over here! Here I am!" But his voice was too faint. Don't forget, he was only a mouse.

After five days with nothing to eat or drink, Doctor De Soto realized he might die. The idea of never ever seeing his dear Deborah again made him so crazy with rage that he seized two bars of his prison and forced his way through.

It was a moonless night.

“I’m coming, Deborah, I’m coming,” he said. Weak as he was, he went stumbling along in the dark—until finally he fell over a rock and fractured his ankle.

“What next?” the dentist asked. He couldn’t drag himself another inch. He was spent.

Doctor De Soto lay on his back, saying his wife's name over and over and wishing he'd never seen Africa, never even heard of it.

But soon after sunrise, thank goodness, a search party happened by. The moment they spotted him, they all came running.

The searchers were horrified by Doctor De Soto's condition. Mindful of his ankle, they eased him onto a stretcher and rushed him back to Mudambo's home.

There, husband and wife clung to each other, kissing and crying.

After wolfing down a cheese sandwich and two cups of strong tea, Doctor De Soto took matters in hand. Seated in a toy wheelchair, he directed his wife as she continued where he had left off.

Mrs. De Soto excavated the remaining decay and skillfully sculpted the piece of walrus tusk contributed by the Museum. Then tooth and tusk were cemented together, and Mudambo had a molar as good as new.

At long last, the elephant was able to smile. And giggle. And guffaw. He swung his wife into a frolicsome fandango. Then he devoured a huge meal of raw vegetables, with a bushel of peanuts on the side.

And what about the De Sotos? The De Sotos were richly rewarded, as Mudambo had promised in his cablegram.

"Bernard," said Mrs. De Soto, "I think we will rest until you're fully recovered. Then how about using these lovely walulus to see a bit more of our beautiful planet?"

"My dear Deborah," said Doctor De Soto, "you must have been reading my mind."